Dear Parents and Educators,

Welcome to Penguin Young Readers! As pa •
know that each child develops at his or her own pace—in terms of
speech, critical thinking, and, of course, reading. Penguin Young
Readers recognizes this fact. As a
book is assigned a traditional eas
Guided Reading Level (A–P). Bot
the right book for your child. Plec
for specific leveling information.
esteemed authors and illustrators
fascinating nonfiction, and more

Bones and the Roller Coaster Mystery

LEVEL **3**

GUIDED
READING **K**
LEVEL

This book is perfect for a **Transitional Reader** who:
• can read multisyllable and compound words;
• can read words with prefixes and suffixes;
• is able to identify story elements (beginning, middle, end, plot, setting,
  characters, problem, solution); and
• can understand different points of view.

Here are some **activities** you can do during and after reading this book:
• Making Inferences: Making an inference involves using what you know
  to make a guess about what you don't know, or reading between the
  lines. For example, on page 18, Bones asks Teddy, his stuffed bear, if
  he's scared of the wooden lions. When Teddy doesn't answer, Bones tells
  us that it is because "lions don't scare Teddy." We can make an inference
  that Bones is not scared of the wooden lions. Find and discuss another
  moment in the story where you can make an inference.
• Make Connections: In this story, the ticket woman says that she once
  found a shoe at the amusement park. Have you ever lost anything? If so,
  what was the strangest thing you've lost? Have you ever found something
  someone else lost? What was the strangest thing you've found?

Remember, sharing the love of reading with a child is the best gift
you can give!

—Bonnie Bader, EdM
   Penguin Young Readers program

*Penguin Young Readers are leveled by independent reviewers applying the standards developed by Irene Fountas
and Gay Su Pinnell in *Matching Books to Readers: Using Leveled Books in Guided Reading*, Heinemann, 1999.

To Lucinda Gunton—happy reading!—DA

For my mom, who early on fostered
my big love of roller coasters
and amusement parks!—BJN

Penguin Young Readers
Published by the Penguin Group
Penguin Group (USA) Inc., 375 Hudson Street, New York, New York 10014, USA
Penguin Group (Canada), 90 Eglinton Avenue East, Suite 700, Toronto, Ontario M4P 2Y3, Canada
(a division of Pearson Penguin Canada Inc.)
Penguin Books Ltd, 80 Strand, London WC2R 0RL, England
Penguin Ireland, 25 St Stephen's Green, Dublin 2, Ireland (a division of Penguin Books Ltd)
Penguin Group (Australia), 707 Collins Street, Melbourne, Victoria 3008, Australia
(a division of Pearson Australia Group Pty Ltd)
Penguin Books India Pvt Ltd, 11 Community Centre, Panchsheel Park, New Delhi—110 017, India
Penguin Group (NZ), 67 Apollo Drive, Rosedale, Auckland 0632, New Zealand
(a division of Pearson New Zealand Ltd)
Penguin Books (South Africa), Rosebank Office Park, 181 Jan Smuts Avenue,
Parktown North 2193, South Africa
Penguin China, B7 Jiaming Center, 27 East Third Ring Road North,
Chaoyang District, Beijing 100020, China

Penguin Books Ltd, Registered Offices: 80 Strand, London WC2R 0RL, England

Text copyright © 2009 by David A. Adler. Illustrations copyright © 2009 by Barbara Johansen Newman.
All rights reserved. First published in 2009 by Viking and in 2010 by Puffin Books, imprints
of Penguin Group (USA) Inc. Published in 2013 by Penguin Young Readers, an imprint
of Penguin Group (USA) Inc., 345 Hudson Street, New York, New York 10014.
Manufactured in China.

The Library of Congress has cataloged the Viking edition
under the following Control Number: 2008021552

ISBN 978-0-14-241687-7   10 9 8 7 6 5 4 3 2

BONES
and the Roller Coaster Mystery

by David A. Adler
illustrated by Barbara Johansen Newman

Penguin Young Readers
An Imprint of Penguin Group (USA) Inc.

Chapter 1
That's a Scary Ride

"Wow!" I said.

"Look at that roller coaster!"
I watched the roller coaster
cars speed across the track.

They went really fast.

"That's a scary ride," Grandpa said.

I took Grandpa's hand.

"Don't worry," I told him.

"I'll be with you."

I take care of Grandpa.

He is never afraid when he is with me.

Sometimes, we solve mysteries.

I'm good at solving mysteries.

I am a great detective.

It was our turn at the ticket booth.

Grandpa told the woman,

"I'd like tickets for games and rides."

He gave her some money.

She gave him some tickets.

"These are good for all the games

and most of the rides," she said.

She opened a large map.

"Here's the Dime Toss," she said.

"It is the best game.

Here is the best ride,

the Merry-Go-Round.

Just stay away from the wooden lions.

They scare me.

There are two roller coasters,"

she said.

"There is a big one and a small one.

The small roller coaster

is for children."

"I'm going on thc big one," I said.

We needed special tickets

for the roller coaster.

Grandpa bought 10 regular tickets

and two roller coaster tickets.

"Thank you," Grandpa said.

The woman gave Grandpa the map.

He folded it and put it in his pocket.

"Now," he said.

"Let's have some fun."

Chapter 2
Teddy Bear

"Try your luck and win a prize,"

the man at the Basketball

Shoot called out.

He had lots of prizes.

One prize was a

big brown bear.

I looked at the bear.

The bear looked at me.

"Let's try that," I said.

Two boys and a woman

were ahead of us.

I told Grandpa,

"Those boys look the same."

"We're twins," one of the boys said.

"I'm Bobby, and he's Barry."

Bobby took five shots.

He missed them all.

Barry took five shots.

He also missed them all.

The woman took five shots

and got two in.

"We have a winner!"

the man called out.

He told the woman

to pick one of the small prizes.

Now it was our turn.

To win the big brown bear,

I would have to get all five shots in.

Grandpa gave the man a ticket.

I took five shots.

I missed them all.

Grandpa gave the man another ticket.

"You can do it," I told Grandpa.

He got all five in.

Grandpa did it!

"Wow!" the basketball man said.

Grandpa told the man he once

played on a basketball team.

Grandpa could pick

 a larger prize.

Grandpa picked the big brown bear

and gave it to me.

I named him Teddy.

We tried the Dime Toss.

We didn't win.

Next, we went on the Merry-Go-Round.

We rode the lions.

They didn't scare us.

"Let's go on the big roller coaster,"

I said.

We walked to the big roller coaster.

I looked up.

It was really big.

People riding the roller coaster
screamed.

It was a scary ride.

Maybe it was too scary.

The roller coaster stopped.

Someone asked, "Can I open my eyes?"

"Yes," the roller coaster man said.

"The ride is over."

Grandpa gave the man two tickets.
The man said, "These are not
roller coaster tickets."
Grandpa showed him all his tickets.
The man shook his head.
Grandpa didn't have
roller coaster tickets.
I told Grandpa, "I think the
ticket woman gave you the
wrong tickets."
We walked to the
ticket booth.

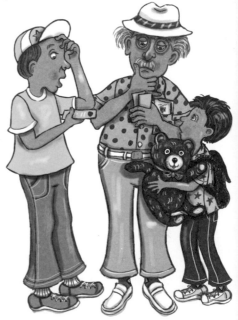

Chapter 3
How Does Someone Lose a Shoe?

The ticket woman was talking

to a young man.

She told him, "The best game

is the Dime Toss.

The best ride is the Merry-Go-Round.

Just stay away from the lions.

They scare me."

I asked Teddy

if the wooden lions scared him.

Teddy didn't answer.

That's because lions don't scare Teddy.

The young man walked away.

It was our turn.

Grandpa said,

"I paid for two roller coaster tickets."

"Did you like the ride?"

the woman asked.

Grandpa told her,

"We didn't ride the roller coaster.

We didn't have the right tickets."

"I gave you ten green tickets,"

the woman said.

"I gave you two blue tickets.

The blue tickets

are for the roller coaster."

All the tickets were the same size.

Only the colors were not the same.

Now Grandpa had just six green tickets.

"Maybe you dropped some,"

the woman said.

"Maybe you lost them.

People lose lots of things.

Last week I found a shoe.

It was near the Dime Toss."

I opened my detective bag.

I took out my glass.

It would help me find the lost tickets.

Grandpa, Teddy, and I looked on
the ground near the ticket booth.
We found candy wrappers.
We didn't find any blue tickets.
"Tell me," the woman said.
"How does someone lose a shoe?"
"I don't know," Grandpa answered.
"I also don't know what happened
to my two roller coaster tickets."

Chapter 4
Grandpa's Smile

Grandpa said, "Maybe I dropped
the tickets at the Basketball Shoot.
Maybe I dropped them at the
Merry-Go-Round or the Dime Toss."
We looked through the park.
We looked for Grandpa's tickets.
While we walked,
I looked at the roller coaster.

It goes much too fast, I thought.

"We can stop looking
for the tickets," I said.
"It is okay if we don't go
on the roller coaster."

"I don't like to lose things,"
Grandpa said.

Then he looked at me and asked,
"Don't you like to solve mysteries?
Well, this is a mystery," Grandpa said.
"I want to know what happened
to my roller coaster tickets."

"You had the tickets," I told

Grandpa, "so I should look at you."

I looked at Grandpa.

Grandpa smiled.

Through my glass his smile

looked *really* big.

I looked at Grandpa's shirt.

Then I saw something

in Grandpa's pocket.

It was the map.

"Hey," I said.

"Maybe the map

will help me find the tickets."

I took the map

from Grandpa's pocket.

I took it out slowly.

I didn't want anything to fall out

of Grandpa's map.

Chapter 5
Wow! What a Ride!

I told Grandpa, "First you got the map.

Then you got the roller coaster tickets.

Maybe you folded them together."

Then I opened the map,

but I didn't find the tickets.

Just then Bobby and Barry walked by.

Just then I solved the mystery.

"Those boys look the same,"
I told Grandpa, "but they're not.
The green and blue tickets
look the same, but they're not.
You bought ten green tickets
and two blue tickets.
That's twelve tickets.
You used two tickets
at the Basketball Shoot.

That left you ten tickets.
You used two at the
Merry-Go-Round
and two at the Dime Toss.
That left you six tickets."
"That's what I have," Grandpa said.
"But you had two blue tickets," I said.
"You must have given someone
the wrong tickets."
We went to the Basketball Shoot.
"Oh no,"
the man told
Grandpa.

"You can win only one prize a day."

"I don't want to play again,"

Grandpa said.

I said, "I think Grandpa gave you

roller coaster tickets."

The man looked through his tickets.

He found Grandpa's two blue tickets.

Grandpa gave the man

two green tickets.

The man gave Grandpa

the two blue tickets.

"Now we can ride the roller coaster,"

Grandpa said.

We walked to the roller coaster.

I looked at Teddy.

Teddy looked at me.

I knew he was scared.

"Grandpa," I said.

"I think the big roller coaster

is too scary for Teddy."

"Yes," Grandpa said.

"I think you are right."

"Maybe," I said, "we should take

Teddy on the smaller one."

That's what we did.

I buckled Teddy in.

"Hold on,"

I told him.

"Don't stand up during the ride."

Teddy didn't stand.

He's a good bear.

Wow!

What a ride!

We had fun

on the smaller roller coaster.

It was scary enough for Teddy.

It was even scary enough for me,

Jeffrey Bones.